D1218469

Monica Hughes

Jan on the Trail

Illustrations by Carlos Freire

FIRST NOVELS

The New Series

Bladen County Public Library
Elizabethtown, N. C. 28337

Formac Publishing Company Limited
Halifax, Nova Scotia

Copyright ©2000 by Monica Hughes

All rights reserved. No part of this book may be reproduced or transmitted in any form or by any means, electronic or mechanical, including photocopying, or by any information storage or retrieval system, without permission in writing from the publisher.

Formac Publishing Company Limited acknowledges the support of the Cultural Affairs Section, of the Nova Scotia Department of Tourism and Culture. We acknowledge the financial support of the Government of Canada through the Book Publishing Industry Development Program (BPIDP) for our publishing activities. We acknowledge the support of the Canada Council for the Arts for our publishing program.

Canadian Cataloguing in Publication Data

Hughes, Monica, 1925-

    Jan on the trail

    (First novels. The new series)
    ISBN 0-88780-502-7 (pbk)
    ISBN 0-88780-503-5 (bound)

I. Freire, Carlos, 1943   I. Title.   II. Series.

PS8565.U34J356 200   jC813'.54   C99-950274-3
PZ7.H8764Jz 2000

Formac Publishing Company
Limited
5502 Atlantic Street
Halifax, NS B3H 1G4

Distributed in the U.S. by
Orca Book Publishers
P.O. Box 468 Custer, WA
U.S.A. 98240-0468

Printed and bound in Canada

Table of Contents

1
Missing, believed stolen

Sarah and I are sharing a strawberry cone. Sarah's brother John says it's disgusting for us to take turns licking.

I say, "Sarah and I are best friends."

Sarah says, "And we're broke. If it bothers you that much, lend us the money for another cone."

"Hah-hah. Fat chance." John goes off to play arcade games with his friends.

Sarah and I walk down the mall, taking turns, each of us

licking the same amount each turn.

We look at the community notice board in the middle of the mall.

Sarah suddenly chokes and sprays wafer crumbs.
"Patch!" she screams.

"Where?" I look around. Patch is my most favourite dog. He's white, with a fat pink tummy and a large black patch on his right ear. Once he lived in the pet store, and Sarah and I used to take him for walks in the park. But last week he was sold.

Sad for Sarah and me. Happy for Joanne, the owner of the pet store, I guess. And definitely happy for whoever got to own him. Lucky kid.

So I look eagerly around when Sarah screams "Patch!".

"Look." Sarah points to the notice board. Then I see it.

LOST
On Thursday May 15th
white puppy with black
patch on right ear
REWARD FOR SAFE RETURN

At the bottom is an address, and in the middle is a photograph of Patch.

"Thursday. That's yesterday," Sarah says.

"Poor Patch. He must be so scared. We've got to find him."

"You mean us? Jan, is this another of your great ideas?"

"He knows us better than anyone except, Joanne," I explain.

"But we don't know where to look," Sarah says. "It's a big city."

"We start there." I point to the address at the bottom of the notice. I copy it down in my notebook.

"But —"

"I've got this notebook. And Mom's got a map of the city. Sarah, we're going to be detectives."

2
Jan and Sarah: detectives

"Let's not waste any time," I say. "We'll go and interview Patch's owner."

We get the map from Mom, and I promise to be back before dark. The address doesn't look very far on the map, but by the time we reach the right street we're hot and tired.

"Never mind. We'll get a bus home," I say.

"No cash," Sarah reminds me.

It *is* difficult being a detective without bus money.

The houses are far apart, with big lawns and two or three-car garages. Walking up the long driveway is kind of scary.

"What are we going to say?" Sarah asks. She's biting her nails, which she only does when she's really nervous.

I pretend I'm not scared. "We'll just say we're friends of Patch and we want to help find him."

The gravel scrunches noisily and I keep thinking someone is going to come to the door and say, "What do *you* want?" But nobody does.

I ring the bell and wait. I ring it again. The door opens slowly and a skinny little kid peeks out.

"Mom says that whatever it is, we don't want any. Thank you," he adds.

He's closing the door in our faces when I gasp, "Wait a minute. It's about Patch."

He stares at me. "Who's Patch?"

3
Who's Patch?

"Who's Patch?" I repeat.
"Why, he's the dog you lost.
There's a poster in the mall."

"You mean Spot." He
comes out and sits on the
step. "Have you found him?"

"No. Not yet." I see tears
in his watery blue eyes.
"That's why we're here," I
say quickly. "To help you find
Patch — I mean Spot."

I tell him our names and
explain that Patch was our
special friend. He says his
name is Carl. They've just
moved into this big house.

He has no friends and he's not in school yet. That's why his mom and dad got him a dog. To be a friend.

"But he ran away." Now he's really crying. I sit on the step beside him and Sarah sits on his other side. We put our arms round him.

"I was playing with him in the garden. I went into the house for some lemonade, and when I came out he was gone."

"I bet he didn't run away. This is a real nice place for a dog. I bet he was kidnapped," I tell him.

"Dog-napped," says Sarah.

"Whatever. Don't worry. We'll find him for you."

The tears stop and Carl gives a huge wet sniff. "Really?"

"Sure." I take my notebook out of my jean jacket. "Friday, May 16th. Interview with Carl. What's your last name, Carl?"

"Forrester. Why?"

"Detectives always write down the details. So he ran away yesterday. What time?"

Carl looks blank.

"Before or after lunch?" Sarah asks. Smart. Little kids don't always know the time, but they sure know meal times.

"It was after lunch. I was thirsty, so I —"

"— went to get some lemonade. What did you do

when you found he was gone?"

"I called his name. Then Mom and I went to all the houses on the street. Then she phoned the pound and that other place ..."

"The SPCA?"

Carl nods. "They said they'd tell us if they found him." He gives another big sniff. "So last night Dad made a poster on the computer and said he'd put it up in the mall."

"He did. Nice picture," Sarah says.

"Dad took a whole bunch of pictures the day we got Spot."

I get to my feet. "Tomorrow's Saturday. Sarah

and I will have the whole day to track the dog-napper."

"Can I come too?" Carl scrambles to his feet.

Sarah and I look at each other. "You're a bit small. You'll get tired."

"No, I won't. Honest."

"Well, you'll have to ask your mom," I say. "Here's our phone numbers." I write them on a page of my notebook and tear it out.

It's a very long walk home. Sarah says, "We should have asked for an advance on the reward so we could get a bus." Then she adds, "You're crazy, Jan MacDonald. Suppose we can't find Patch?"

I walk on. I'm thinking the same thing.

4
The Dog-napper

That evening Carl's mother calls our house, but Mom's working late, so Gran takes the call.

"Mrs. Forrester? ... Oh, I see ... Yes, I would say Jan is both resourceful *and* responsible. But she's a bit too young for baby-sitting ... Oh, not baby-sitting ... Carl said she was a *detective?*"

They talk some more. She puts the phone down and looks at me over her glasses. "Jan MacDonald, what are you up to?"

I explain about Patch and how Sarah and I are going to find him. Gran's eyes twinkle and I know it's okay. She gives me some money for bus fares and emergencies. She even makes sandwiches for us to take.

"A hungry detective is good for nothing," she says.

* * *

Early on Saturday morning Sarah and I take the bus to Carl's house. He's sitting on the steps waiting for us. He's wearing a small backpack and a sun-hat.

His mother comes out onto the porch as we scrunch up the driveway. "I called the pet store and the owner says you're very responsible. Thank you both. Carl really misses his new friend."

I know what she means. I miss Patch too.

I take out the map and explain our plan. "North of here it's mostly country. South is where the mall is. If Patch did run away, he'd likely go that way."

"You mean Spot, don't you," Mrs. Forrester says.

"Whatever." I don't tell her about my dog-napping idea.

"I've told Carl to call me on my cell phone once in a while. I'll drive around up north. Maybe he's on one of the acreages."

We say goodbye and set out. Every once in a while Carl stops and calls out, "Spot, where are you?"

There's no answer.

Whenever we hear a dog barking we stop and check. We ask everyone we meet if they've seen a fat white puppy with a pink tummy and a black patch on his right ear. Nobody has.

When Carl is tired we stop in a little park that has a drinking fountain. We decide to eat our sandwiches. Carl has his in his backpack.

I write in my notebook everything we've done so far. It's not very encouraging. When Carl feels better we go on walking. The houses are

Bladen County Public Library
Elizabethtown. N. C. 28337

close together now and kind
of shabby.

I stop a man walking *his*
dog and ask him about Patch.

He shakes his head.
"Haven't seen him. You could
ask over there. They have a
whole bunch of dogs. Too
many, if you ask me."

I'm about to go over to the
house he points to when a
tall man comes out. He's
wearing a T-shirt that says
NO FEAR, and jeans with a
tear in the leg. His hair is long
and scraggly. He's holding a
garbage bag filled with
something lumpy.

He slings it over his
shoulder and walks down the
street. He has a very bouncy
walk. With every bounce I

can hear a small "yip" from inside the garbage bag.

I clutch Sarah's and Carl's arms. "The dog-napper," I whisper.

"What'll we do?"

"Follow him. Don't let him out of our sight."

This is not easy. He's walking fast. He turns one corner and then another. Carl is trying to keep up.

We pass a bus stop with a wooden seat. "Sit and wait for us," I tell him. "Don't move or you'll get lost."

"We're already lost," Sarah says as we hurry on.

"We've got the map," I pant. "Quick. Round this corner."

We run around the corner. The dog-napper has vanished.

5
Chop-stick time

We stare at the empty road.
My heart is thumping. Where
did he go?

"He can't have flown away,"
Sarah says practically. "He
must be in one of these stores."

We walk slowly along,
peering in every window.
There a store that sells vacuum
cleaners. A Chinese restaurant
with a tank full of enormous
goldfish. A thrift store with
second-hand clothes hanging in
the window.

I stop suddenly and Sarah
bumps into me.

"Look!" I hiss.

The man is emptying the garbage bag onto the counter. Out tumbles a bundle of clothes. Some books. A big stuffed dog. It rolls off the counter and goes "Yip" as it hits the floor.

"That's certainly not Patch," says Sarah crossly.

"And he's not a dog-napper after all." I feel really dumb. We walk back to where Carl is waiting patiently at the bus stop.

When I tell him we've been following a stuffed toy, he's not as upset as I expect. He's got something else on his mind.

"I need to go to the bathroom," he says.

I look around. The restaurant is our only hope. It seems like a long time since we ate our sandwiches. Gran gave me emergency money and this is an emergency.

"Let's eat," I say.

While Carl is in the bathroom we order egg rolls and lemon chicken. I write down the cost in my notebook.

"Why are you doing that?" Sarah asks.

"Expenses," I tell her. "Detectives always list their expenses."

"Did you write down about the dog-napper that wasn't?" she asks.

I give her a look. Then Carl comes back and we eat lunch. For a little guy he's

got a big appetite. When we've finished he asks the owner if he can use the phone to call his mom. I explain about Patch.

"Have *you* seen him?" we ask.

"Maybe. Is he small and white?"

"With a patch on his right ear," I add eagerly.

He nods. "Thursday evening. He was sniffing around the garbage. I gave him a bit of chicken and he went off." He points down the road.

I spread my map out on the table and ask the owner to show us where his restaurant is. He puts his finger on the map and I mark the place with an X.

"And he went that way." He points. I draw an arrow.

Carl comes back from the phone. "Mom says nobody's seen him." He sniffs.

"But this man has," I tell him. "Cheer up, Carl. We're on the trail."

6
Hot on the trail

The arrow on my map points to the mall. "I bet Patch is going back to Joanne."

"It's an awfully long way," says Sarah, doubtfully.

I remind her that dogs have an amazing sense of smell.

"I mean, it's an awfully long way to walk. Especially for Carl."

"I'm okay," says Carl. "Let's go."

Small but spunky, I think. We set out along the road,

looking for a small white dog as we go.

"Spot! Come here, Spot!" Carl calls at every corner. There is no answering bark.

We ask everyone we meet if they've seen a small white puppy with a black patch on one ear. Nobody has.

We walk on. The map makes the road look straight, but there's a surprise ahead. A new building is going up, right in the middle of what used to be an open space.

In front of us is a huge square hole, the size of an underground parking lot. Directly in front of it is a high, mesh fence with barbed wire on top. A big sign says DANGER. KEEP OUT.

We stop and argue whether we should turn left or right. I think I hear a whimper.

"Shh… Listen."

"Is it Spot? Spot, are you down there?" Carl shouts.

Silence.

"You're hearing things, Jan," says Sarah.

"Patch!" I yell. "Patch, is that you?"

Suddenly there's barking and whimpering. I can hear claws scrabbling against the side of the pit, but it's obvious Patch can't get out.

And we can't get in to help him.

"What are we going to do?" Sarah asks.

The site is deserted. There are notices on the fence.

"Look," I say, "Here's the phone number for the company that's putting up the building."

"Only it's Saturday. Nobody will be there. Rats!" says Sarah.

We look at each other in despair.

"My mom says if you're in trouble ask a policewoman," Carl says.

"That's very smart," Sarah tells him.

I stare at the map. It's got little flags that say H for hospital and S for school. There's a green one that says P. P is for parking. Rats again!

Sarah looks over my shoulder and points. "The

little *blue* flags say P for police station. Maybe ..."

"There's one!"

We start walking again.

7
Police to the rescue

It's five very long blocks to the police station. It's a tiny room with three chairs in front of the counter, and a desk and chair behind it.

Seated at the desk is a policewoman.

"Oh, please, can you help us —"

"It's my dog, Spot —"

"Fallen into the hole where the new building is going up."

We all talk at once and the policewoman makes us stop and explain one at a time.

Then she nods and picks up the phone. "I'll call the security company. They'll send someone out to unlock the gate and rescue your dog — what's his name again?"

"Patch," I say.

"Spot," says Carl.

"Which is it? Spot or Patch? Whose dog is he? Or is this just a game?" She frowns and puts the phone down. We explain all over again.

She picks up the phone again and dials a number. It must be the security company. "A man will be right over to unlock the gate. You'd better go back to the site and tell him what's happened."

"May I phone my mom first?" Carl asks.

The policewoman hands over the phone. Carl talks to his mom. Then he looks at me and says, "Mom wants to know where we the building site is. She says she'll come and pick us up."

I look at the map and read out the number of the street and avenue. We run the five long blocks back to the building site.

"Patch, are you still there?"

I hear a faint whimper.

"Someone's coming to rescue you, Spot," Carl yells.

We sit on the sidewalk with our backs against the fence and rest our tired feet. I feel as if we've been walking for ever.

Finally a car pulls up and a man in a blue uniform gets out. He walks over to us.

"What's the problem?" he asks.

We explain. "He's white with a black patch on his ear," I add.

He unhooks a bunch of keys from his belt, chooses one and unlocks the gate in the fence. He makes us wait outside while he goes to the edge and looks over.

"Hello, little fellow," he says.

Patch whimpers and lets out one small bark. He sounds awfully hoarse.

"How are you going to get him out of there?" I ask.

"There's a ladder over here. Just you wait outside." He climbs out of sight.

We wait. And wait. Carl grabs my hand. His is all sweaty.

"It's going to be all right," I tell him.

Finally we see the top of the man's head. Then his face. He's smiling. Then his shoulders and chest.

Tucked safely into the front of his uniform jacket is a small fat puppy.

"Patch!" I yell.

"Spot!" yells Carl.

"Make up your minds," says the man. "No wonder the poor dog's confused."

He holds Patch in his arms with a finger hooked under his collar. "Have you got his leash?"

Carl takes off his backpack and looks inside. He pulls out a new, bright red leash.

The man clips it to Patch's collar and hands the other end to Carl. "Hold tight now. Don't let him run away again. He might not be so lucky next time."

"How do you suppose he got down there?" I ask the security man.

"Wriggled under the fence," the man says. "Somebody'd thrown down the remains of a hamburger. I guess he was hungry enough to go after it."

He looks at Patch, in Carl's arms, and laughs. "I thought he was supposed to be a small white dog?"

He turns to lock the gate.

"Thank you very much for saving him," Sarah and I say.

"You're welcome. Have a nice day!"

"Oh, we will. It's a wonderful day!"

8
A wonderful day

We sit on the sidewalk, our backs against the fence. Poor Patch! He's filthy dirty, covered with yellow clay. His paws look sore. When I touch them he whimpers.

I know what he feels like. My feet are killing me and I've got sandals on.

A long white Cadillac pulls up in front of us.

"Mom!" Carl scrambles to his feet. "We found him."

"So I see. Let's go home and give him a bath and a good meal."

Carl climbs into the back of the car, Patch in his arms. Sarah and I stand at the curb, hesitating.

"Come on, you two. Hop in. Once Spot is clean and fed we'll have tea. Then I'll drive you home."

We climb into the back of the car and lie back. I sigh. Sarah sighs. Neither of us has ridden in a white Cadillac before. It feels wonderful. My feet hurt so much, a ride in a wheelbarrow would feel good. But this is special.

Carl takes us round to the back of the house. The garden there is even bigger than in front. There are trees and shrubs and flowers everywhere.

Carl pulls an old plastic baby bath onto the patio and we fill it with warm water. Sarah and I we put Patch in and shampoo his white hair. We gently wash the clay from between his toes. Poor Patch! He whimpers but he doesn't try to get away. I guess he's too tired.

Sarah and I wrap him in a towel and take turns to pat him dry. Then Carl comes out carefully carrying a dish of water and a dish of puppy chow.

Patch jumps out of our arms and eats and drinks until the dishes are empty. He gives a big sigh and lies down in the shade of a bush and goes to sleep.

"That's the best thing for him," Mrs. Forrester says. "Monday we'll take him to the vet and see if he needs ointment for his paws."

She has brought out a tea trolley loaded with cakes and sandwiches and milk and lemonade. Carl digs in right away. You'd think he hadn't had a bite in hours.

I'll always remember today for the most walking and the most eating I've ever done.

When we're full we just sit there, half asleep in the afternoon sun.

9
Spot or Patch?

Patch wakes up. He blinks and looks around as if he can't believe that he's safely home.

"Hey, Spot," Carl says lovingly.

Patch ignores him. He licks his sore paws.

"Hey, Patch," I say. "How're you doing?"

He pricks up one floppy black ear and limps over to lick my hand.

Mrs. Forrester is watching. She looks at Carl and smiles.

"You know, Carl, I think you and I made a bad mistake. This dog isn't Spot. He never was Spot. That's why he didn't come home when you called. His name is Patch."

Carl looks from his mother to Patch and back again. She nods.

"Hey, Patch," Carl says softly.

Patch limps over and licks his hand.

Now everything is A-okay. I write: *mission complete* in my notebook. Then I stand up and stretch. "I guess we'd better get home before our parents start worrying."

"I'll drive you," Mrs. Forrester says. "We'll leave

Carl and Patch to get to know each other again."

We say goodbye and walk around to the driveway. We climb into the front seat of the car with Mrs. Forrester.

"You're welcome to come and visit any time," she says as she drives. "Carl and Patch will love to see you."

The car stops in front of Gran's house and we get out.

Mrs. Forrester looks in her purse and takes out two white envelopes. "Here," she says. "I can't thank you enough for rescuing Patch. Carl was a very sad little boy without him."

She drives off. Sarah and I look at each other. Then we tear open our envelopes.

There is a crisp new twenty-dollar bill in mine. There's a crisp new twenty-dollar bill in Sarah's.

"Wow!" we say together.

"How are you going to spend it?" we ask each other.

We think about it. It's almost like winning the lottery.

Then I get this great idea. "I think maybe …" I start to say.

But that's another story …

Look for these New First Novels!

Meet Duff
Duff's Monkey Business
Duff the Giant Killer

Meet Jan
Jan on the Trail
Jan and Patch
Jan's Big Bang

Meet Lilly
Lilly's Good Deed
Lilly to the Rescue

Meet Robyn
Robyn Looks for Bears
Robyn's Want Ad
Shoot for the Moon, Robyn

Meet Morgan
Morgan's Secret
Morgan and the Money
Morgan Makes Magic

Meet Carrie
Carrie's Crowd
Go For It, Carrie

Meet all the kids in the
First Novel Series

Meet Arthur
Arthur Throws a Tantrum
Arthur's Dad
Arthur's Problem Puppy

Meet Fred
Fred and the Flood
Fred and the Stinky Cheese
Fred's Dream Cat

Meet Leo
Leo and Julio

Meet the Loonies
Loonie Summer
The Loonies Arrive

Meet Maddie
Maddie Tries To Be Good
Maddie in Trouble
Maddie in Hospital
Maddie Goes to Paris
Maddie in Danger
Maddie in Goal
Maddie Wants Music
That's Enough Maddie!

Meet Marilou
Marilou on Stage

Meet Max
Max the Superhero

Meet Mikey
Mikey Mite's Best Present
Good For You, Mikey Mite!
Mikey Mite Goes to School
Mikey Mite's Big Problem

Meet Mooch
Missing Mooch
Mooch Forever
Hang On, Mooch!
Mooch Gets Jealous
Mooch and Me

Meet Raphael
Video Rivals

Meet the Swank Twins
The Swank Prank
Swank Talk

Meet Will
Will and His World

Formac Publishing Company Limited
5502 Atlantic Street, Halifax, Nova Scotia B3H 1G4
Orders: 1-800-565-1975 Fax: (902) 425-0166